INVERCLYDE LIBRARIES

Horse of Fire

To Trina, thanks for all your horse expertise,
over many years and many books.

First published in 2016 by Bloomsbury Education,
an imprint of Bloomsbury Publishing Plc
50 Bedford Square, London, WC1B 3DP

www.bloomsbury.com

Bloomsbury is a registered trademark
of Bloomsbury Publishing Plc

A CIP catalogue for this book is available from the British Library

ISBN 978-1-4729-2096-6

Printed by CPI Group (UK) Ltd, Croydon CR0 4YY

1 3 5 7 9 10 8 6 4 2

Horse of Fire

horse stories from around the world

LARI DON

BLOOMSBURY EDUCATION
AN IMPRINT OF BLOOMSBURY
LONDON   OXFORD   NEW YORK   NEW DELHI   SYDNEY

Contents

Pegasus and the Monsters
Greek myth

Heroes are often more trouble than they're worth, especially to their horses.

Perseus was a typical Greek hero: tall, strong, handsome and good with long sharp weapons. Like many Greek heroes, he was the son of a god. Perseus wanted to prove himself worthy to his father Zeus, so he set off on a quest, to kill the monster Medusa.

Medusa hadn't been born a monster. She'd been a human girl until a powerful goddess, who was jealous of Medusa's beauty, transformed her hair into snakes and her eyes into weapons. Now anyone who looked Medusa in the eye was turned to stone, so she didn't have many friends and spent a lot of time chatting to statues.

But Perseus was on a quest, so he was determined to kill her. He crept up on her, he watched her in the reflection of his shiny shield and waited for his chance, then he sliced off her head.

As Medusa died, her only child was born, from the blood-soaked earth under her fallen body, and from her pain and loneliness.

Medusa's child was a winged black horse called Pegasus, who was furious at the death of his mother. He struggled up from the pool of mud and blood, and flexed his wide feathered wings. Then he rose into the air and swooped down to take revenge on his mother's killer, who was calmly dropping Medusa's severed head into a sturdy bag.

Pegasus attacked with his hooves and his teeth.

But Pegasus had only just been born, and Perseus had trained as a warrior all his life.

So Perseus stepped to one side, let Pegasus rush past him, and leapt onto the horse's back.

He tugged on the horse's mane with his hands, he squeezed the horse's flanks with his legs and he jabbed the horse's belly with his heels. Perseus sat on this magnificent flying beast and said, "Take me home, horsie, quick as you like."

Pegasus obeyed, because the hero was resting a sharp sword on his neck and twisting heavy fists in his mane. So the winged horse glided over the sea towards Perseus's home.

On the way, Perseus spotted a girl chained to a rock. "Fly down," he ordered, with a painful jerk of his hands. "This looks like another job for a hero…"

As Pegasus circled above the rock, the girl called up to Perseus, "I've been chained here as a sacrifice to the sea monster Cetus. You look like a proper hero on your fabulous winged horse, so I'd be really grateful if you could save me." She shouted, even louder, "Also, I'm a princess and I'll marry you if you rescue me."

"Right, horsie," said Perseus. "Ready to make me a hero all over again?"

The waters surged below them and a massive scaly monster rose from the deep. Perseus forced Pegasus to fly close to its stinking fishy fangs, then Perseus pulled Medusa's head from the bag and turned Cetus to stone. The monster became a cliff-sided island in the sea.

Then the hero forced Pegasus to land on the rock beside the girl. He jumped off the horse and gave the chained girl a kiss. "Let me take you home," he said.

But he couldn't take her home on Pegasus, because the horse had flown away as soon as Perseus leapt off his back.

Pegasus flew to a clear pool high in the mountains to wash off the rotting-fish smell of the sea monster's breath and the sweat of the hero who'd killed his mother then treated him like a servant.

Pegasus decided to have no more to do with heroes.

But heroes are hard to avoid.

Just as Perseus was settling down with

his princess, another hero was starting his monster-killing career.

Bellerophon was even taller and even more skilled at fighting than Perseus. He was fast and strong, charming and handsome. He sang in tune, wrote poetry and rescued kittens from trees.

He was such a wonderful hero that his own king was afraid of him. Afraid that one day the people would decide they'd prefer Bellerophon to be their king. So the king wrote a note, sealed it and handed it to Bellerophon. "I have a vital mission for you. Please deliver this to the king of the kingdom to the west."

Bellerophon put on his armour, his sword and his charming smile, and headed off on his royal mission.

He arrived at the palace and presented the note to the western king, who offered Bellerophon refreshments, then opened the note just as Bellerophon was dipping his bread in oil and taking his first bite.

The note said: "My brother king, the messenger who brings this note is such an impressive hero that he is a danger to all kings. Please do me a favour and kill him."

The western king looked up at Bellerophon, who smiled and said something charming and polite about the food.

The western king read the note again and realised he'd made a mistake, offering the messenger a meal before reading the message. Bellerophon was now the king's guest, he had eaten the king's food at the king's table. So by the laws of hospitality, the king couldn't kill him. Guest-killing was a terrible crime, punished by the gods.

But the western king wanted to do this favour for his neighbour, because he understood how inconvenient heroes could be. He had to find a way to cause Bellerophon's death, without actually killing Bellerophon himself.

"Your own king thinks a great deal of you," said the western king.

Bellerophon smiled. "Oh, you know how it is, when you're a hero."

The king said, "You must be a wonderful slayer of monsters."

Bellerophon shrugged modestly. "I've killed a few monsters. Or is it a few dozen? Or perhaps a few hundred! I lose count."

"So you find monster-killing easy? That's interesting, because I have a nasty monster in my kingdom…"

"I've eaten your bread," said Bellerophon. "So if you want me to do you a favour, just ask."

"Then I ask you to slay our local monster, the chimera."

"A monster I haven't heard of! I like a challenge. Tell me more."

The western king smiled. "The chimera has a lion's body, with a lion's head and teeth at the front. It also has a goat's head on its back, with sword-sharp horns. And instead of a tail, it has a serpent's body, head and fangs.

"It has three heads, but four ways of killing. It can bite as a lion, it can gore as a goat, it can poison as a snake and it can breathe fire at you, from any of its three mouths, as you run away."

"I won't run away," said Bellerophon confidently. "I will kill this chimera for you."

But Bellerophon wasn't a stupid hero. He didn't jump straight into a fight; he did his research first. So he watched the chimera for a day and a night, to work out the best way to defeat it.

He noticed that the chimera could watch in front and behind at the same time, and that the three heads took turns sleeping. It would be impossible to sneak up on his target. This would not be an easy monster to kill.

However, as he spied on the monster, he realised that the chimera's three heads never looked up. The chimera watched the ground but not the sky. It could be taken by surprise with an attack from the air.

But how could he attack from the air?

Then Bellerophon remembered a story he'd once heard about a fabulous flying horse who'd helped a hero defeat a sea monster and save a princess.

So he chatted charmingly with a few dryads, the spirits of trees, and with a few naiads, the spirits of water, and learnt the location of Pegasus's favourite pool.

Bellerophon visited his weapons-maker to order sharp-tipped arrows and a heavy-tipped spear, and visited his saddler to order a strong bridle, decorated with jewels and gold.

Then he hid by the pool, with the golden bridle in his hand. He waited patiently for days, until one morning the magnificent black horse swooped down from the sky, gliding to earth on his gleaming wings.

Pegasus landed lightly on his hooves and trotted to the water. When the horse lowered his head to drink, Bellerophon leapt on him and flung the bridle over his nose and neck.

Pegasus had a bossy hero on his back, again.

He was forced to fly straight towards a monster, again.

Bellerophon and Pegasus dived out of the clouds towards the chimera, who was looking forwards and backwards and to the sides, but not looking up at the sky.

So the attack was a complete surprise.

Bellerophon fired three arrows in quick succession, hitting the lion, the goat and the snake. But he wasn't used to firing from a swooping horse, so he hit their necks not their heads, and he only wounded them.

The hero kept attacking with more arrows, forcing Pegasus to fly closer to the chimera.

Now the chimera fought back: biting, goring, striking and breathing fire.

But the teeth, the horns, the poison and the flames didn't hurt Bellerophon, high up on Pegasus's back. They hurt Pegasus. The horse's head was further forward, his legs were lower down, his wings were the widest target. So the horse was cut and bruised and burnt every time Bellerophon forced him towards the vicious heads of the chimera.

The hero ordered the winged horse to go nearer and nearer the fire and the fangs. Just as Pegasus was sure he was about to be roasted and eaten, Bellerophon jabbed his heavy-tipped spear at the lion's mouth.

He pushed the spear right down the lion's throat. The lion roared, the lion breathed fire, and the lion's own flames melted the tip of the spear.

The specially designed spearhead was made

of lead, which liquefied in the heat, so a river of molten lead flowed down the lion's throat, into the belly shared by all three heads.

The hot metal choked them all.

The three heads coughed and roared and bleated and hissed and coughed again. The chimera fell silent and fell to the ground.

Bellerophon leapt off Pegasus's back and hacked off the three heads, to prove the monster was dead.

Pegasus didn't want to carry more severed heads. He shook his own head, to dislodge the golden bridle, then he took off right over Bellerophon's head, and flew far away from Greece, to somewhere he hoped there would be no heroes to boss him about.

But there are heroes and heroines everywhere.

So if you're in training to be a heroine or a hero, and if you ever need a flying horse to defeat a monster, I might be able to tell you where Pegasus drinks his water now. But you'd have to promise to ask him politely to join you on your quest, rather than simply leap on his back and kick him in the ribs, like those olden-day heroes.

The Golden Horse
Gambian folktale

Galonchi owned a pretty gold-coloured horse, with shiny golden flanks and a pale golden mane and tail. His wife owned a pretty pair of gold earrings, bright hoops hanging from her small dark ears.

That was all they had, apart from each other, because they never had any money.

One day Galonchi said, "We'll have to sell the horse or sell the earrings, or even both, so we can eat this month."

His wife said, "But if we sell everything we

own and buy food with the money, then when the food runs out, we won't have anything left to sell."

Galonchi nodded. "So we need to sell the horse and the earrings for enough money to buy food and also to buy another horse and more earrings." He sat and he thought. He looked at the sunlight shining on his horse's flanks, and at the sunlight shining on his wife's earrings.

Then he smiled. "We need to make them more valuable than an ordinary horse or ordinary earrings. We can do that by putting them together."

His wife laughed. "A horse, wearing earrings? That won't sell!"

Galonchi grinned. "Give me one of your earrings." He dipped the gold earring in the last of the salt in his pouch, then he placed it on the palm of his hand and offered it to the horse.

The horse flicked her ears in surprise, but she licked the earring, liked the salt and swallowed the golden circle.

"Hey!" said his wife. "That was my earring! Now it's gone!"

"No, it hasn't," said Galonchi. "It hasn't gone forever. It will reappear eventually. Now let's visit the chief."

·They walked to the nearest village, leading the pretty golden horse, and they told the gatekeeper they had something wonderful to show the chief. While they waited to see him, Galonchi fed his wife's other earring to the horse.

They were admitted to the chief's compound and led into the centre of his big courtyard. The chief was sitting with his family in the shade of a wide tree. "So, Galonchi, what do you have to show me?"

"A magic horse, sir!"

"What does she do? Does she fly, does she speak, does she fight dragons?"

"Wait and see," said Galonchi.

The chief and his family watched the horse. Soon the whole village had heard about the magic horse, so they all crowded round the edge of the courtyard to wait and watch too.

Was the horse going to sing, or dance, or breathe fire, or add up sums, or write in the dust with her hooves?

The horse just lifted her tail and – *plop plop squelch* – dropped a big heap of steaming horse dung onto the ground.

The chief laughed. "That's not magic. My own horses can do that!"

"Ah," said Galonchi, "but can they do this?"

He poked at the pile of smelly dung with a stick. And there, in the middle of the dung, was a gleam of gold.

"This is the Horse of the Golden Dung," he announced. "She is made of gold, so every pile of dung will contain a little gift of gold for her owner."

"Oooh!" said the chief. "I want that horse. I want to be her owner. Will you sell her to me?"

"But my wife and I love this little horse…"

The chief said, "I'll give you anything."

Galonchi frowned, then nodded. "If you give me the price of one hundred ordinary horses, I will sell you the Horse of the Golden Dung."

"Perhaps this is a trick," said the wife

sitting by the chief's right hand. "Perhaps Galonchi dropped in the gold when he stirred the mess with that stick."

"You are wise, my first wife," said the chief. "But I'm not easily fooled. Put Galonchi and his wife as my guests over there." He pointed to the east side of the courtyard. "Put the horse as far from them as possible over there." He pointed to the west side of the courtyard. "And we'll see what's in the next pile of dung."

So Galonchi and his wife sat happily on one side of the courtyard, eating the chief's stew, while the horse stood happily on the other side, eating the chief's hay. And everyone waited.

Then the horse lifted her pretty golden tail and – *plop plop squelch* – she dropped another pile of warm dung, onto the toes of the chief, who was standing right behind her.

The chief poked the dung with a stick and there, in the middle of the steaming brown pile, was the gleam of gold.

"This *is* the Horse of the Golden Dung," he cried. "And she will be mine!"

He handed Galonchi a heavy bag of silver coins, enough to buy one hundred ordinary horses. ("Or," Galonchi whispered to his wife, "fifty horses and fifty pairs of earrings.")

They said goodbye to the pretty golden horse, left the courtyard and started walking away from the village.

The chief stood behind the horse with a great big smile, waiting eagerly for the next steaming pile of dung to land – *plop plop squelch* – on his toes.

Galonchi said to his wife, "Shall we head for the next village ruled by a gullible chief, and buy another horse and another pair of earrings on the way?"

"No," said his wife. "Let's buy an elephant. That will make an even bigger *PLOP PLOP SQUELCH…*"

Riddling for the Foal

Russian folktale

Once there was a poor farmer, whose only horse, a fine mare, gave birth to a beautiful foal. But the mare was at the edge of the farmer's one small field when she gave birth, and the long-legged foal wobbled off his land and fell asleep under his neighbour's cart.

His neighbour, a rich farmer, laughed. "Look, my cart has given birth to a foal! How lucky for me. I will keep the foal, and sell it when it is grown."

The poor farmer said, "Don't be daft.

My mare gave birth to that foal, so the foal is mine."

"The foal is on my land, under my cart, and I'm keeping it," said the rich farmer. "There's nothing you can do about it."

The poor farmer trudged back to his cottage, where his young daughter asked, "How's the mare? Has she foaled yet?"

The poor farmer told her the foal had been born and was healthy, but he also told her how their neighbour had claimed the foal as his own.

His daughter laughed. "He claims that his cart gave birth to the foal? What nonsense! Any sensible judge will rule for you and give us back our foal. You must ask the tsar to give you justice."

So the poor farmer went to the young tsar's palace, just a mile up the road, and asked for justice.

The tsar summoned the rich farmer to bring the foal before him, and told both farmers to make their claim to the foal.

The rich farmer said, "The foal was found

on my land, under my cart. It's obvious the cart gave birth to the foal and therefore the foal belongs to me. My neighbour certainly can't prove otherwise."

The poor farmer said, "But... but... but... surely it's obvious that the mare gave birth to the foal. That's just common sense."

The young tsar hid a grin with a stern frown. "Common sense and legal logic are not the same thing. I will set you both a test, to decide who gets the foal. I will ask three riddles, and the farmer who gives the best answers tomorrow morning will have proved his right to this fine long-legged foal.

"You must answer these three questions:
What is the strongest thing in the world?
What is the fattest thing in the world?
And what is the hardest thing to find?"

The two farmers, rich and poor, went home to puzzle over the answers, leaving the disputed foal to be cared for in the tsar's stables.

The rich farmer discussed the answers over a three-course meal of soup, meat and cake with his wife. The poor farmer discussed the answers over a plate of bread and cheese with his daughter.

"How will I ever answer those riddles?" said the poor farmer. "Whenever I look at the tsar, my knees go weak and I start to stutter."

"I will give you the answers," said his daughter. "Speak them loud and clear, and if you feel nervous, just imagine me beside you, holding your hand and giving you courage."

So, the next day, the young tsar asked both farmers:

"What is the strongest thing in the world?"

The rich farmer said, "My grey stallion, because he can pull a cart with my wife AND both her big sisters in it."

The poor farmer said, "The wind, because it can knock over the tallest tree." The tsar raised his eyebrows and smiled.

"What is the fattest thing in the world?"

The rich farmer said, "My spotted pig, because she eats more than me every single day, and she'll make good eating herself one day."

The poor farmer said, "The earth, because

she feeds all of us, every day." The tsar looked out at the fields beyond his palace and nodded.

"And what is the hardest thing to find?"

The rich farmer said, "My black cat, because I'm always tripping over her in the dark."

The poor farmer said, "The hardest thing to find is justice from a foolish judge."

The tsar breathed in sharply. "Is that your own answer, farmer, or did someone else put you up to that impertinent reply? Did someone else suggest all your smart answers?"

The farmer stuttered, "Yes, but… but… but… she meant no harm…"

"Who? Who gave you these answers?"

"My daughter, sir. She's still just a girl, sir, and she wants our foal back, and she was only trying to help."

"Let's see how smart she really is. I will set another riddle, and unless your daughter can transform herself into the answer, I will give the foal to your neighbour, who does seem to have a clear legal claim."

The tsar set one more riddle:

"She must visit my palace

Neither on horseback nor on foot
Neither clothed nor naked
Neither bearing a gift nor empty-handed
And greet me neither indoors nor outdoors."

The poor farmer walked home, almost in tears, and told his daughter that she had to become the answer to another of the young tsar's riddles.

He repeated the riddle to her and she laughed. "If the tsar wants to play games, I can play games too."

The next day the girl set off towards the palace, riding on the back of a goat, wrapped firmly in a large fishing net and carrying a dove in her cupped hands. She stopped the goat in the doorway of the palace. When the tsar arrived to meet his guest, she held the dove up as if to present it to him, then let it go. The dove fluttered away.

"I am here," she said. "On a goat, rather than on horseback or on foot. I'm not wearing clothes, but this net means I'm not naked either. I didn't come empty-handed, because that would be rude, but I doubt you'll be able to catch that dove and keep it as a pet. And I greet you, great tsar, from your grand doorway, which is neither indoors nor outdoors. So, I am the answer to your riddle. Now will you give my father his foal?"

The young tsar laughed. "I've not yet made my judgement on that complex case. But I'll be more likely to favour your father's version of events, if you can take these dozen new-laid eggs home with you today, hatch them out tonight and bring me back the fully fledged geese tomorrow morning."

She smiled. "I will hatch the eggs, if you promise to feed the geese on fish harvested from the trees of your orchard."

The tsar frowned. "Fish? Growing on trees? Don't be foolish!"

"I'm no more foolish than a man who believes a cart can give birth to a foal. And I'm certainly not as foolish as a tsar who wastes time amusing himself with daft riddles while a poor family loses their horse."

The tsar nodded. "You're right. I've been playing with words when I should have been solving problems, giving out riddles when I should have been giving out justice. I'm sorry. Of course your father has the right to the foal his mare gave birth to." He turned to his servants. "Give the farmer his foal, and enough money to buy fodder for the rest of the horse's life."

He looked back at the girl. "But I do like riddles and I do admire someone who can answer them. Please, would you visit the palace again, so we can ask each other more riddles?"

"Do I have to arrive on a bad-tempered goat, wearing a smelly fishing net, carrying a pecky bird in my hands, then spend the visit in a draughty doorway?"

"No, you may arrive and dress as you please, and you will be my honoured guest."

So the girl visited the young tsar every week, and as the foal grew, so did she. After they'd solved many riddles together, the tsar asked her one straightforward question. He asked her if she would like to be his tsarina.

I can't tell you if she said yes, or no, or answered with a riddle.

But I can tell you that the long-legged foal grew up strong and beautiful and lived happily ever after.

The Horse of Fire
Finnish myth

Lemminkäinen, the hero, wanted to marry the daughter of Louhi, the old woman of the forest, so Louhi set him a task to win her daughter's hand. She ordered Lemminkäinen to find the Fire Horse of Hiisi, the flaming young horse of the meadows, then catch him, tame him and ride him to her gate.

So Lemminkäinen made a silver jewelled bridle and set off to tame the horse of fire.

He walked for days to reach the meadows of Hiisi, then he walked for days through the meadows, searching for the horse. He found burnt hoofprints on the ground, but he couldn't find the young horse among the rolling hills.

He climbed a nearby mountain and watched the meadows, looking for the burning mane of the Fire Horse of Hiisi.

At last he saw a bright light in the distance. He leapt down the mountain and ran towards it.

He found a chestnut horse with a mane of gold and red flame, little sparks dancing all over his flanks, a long burning tail and smouldering black hooves.

The young horse looked at the hero without fear. Lemminkäinen smiled at the horse and held out his hand. The young horse sniffed him. Lemminkäinen grimaced as the horse's skin scorched his fingers.

The horse was gorgeous, strong, friendly and curious. But he was also covered in blisteringly hot fire.

While the horse was on fire, Lemminkäinen couldn't ride him or even touch him.

So the hero raised his hands to the sky and

called on the god Ukku for help. "Lord Ukku, please send hail to douse these flames."

Dark clouds galloped across the sky, covered the sun and began to throw down hailstones. Tiny specks of hail, to put out the sparks on the young horse's flanks. Hailstones the size of teeth, to put out the flames on his tail. Hailstones the size of fists, to put out the flames on his mane.

As the icy hailstones neared the horse of fire, they melted and dripped onto the flames. The fire burnt lower, then died. The Fire Horse of Hiisi became a soggy brown horse, standing sad and bedraggled in the hail-crushed flowers of the meadow.

As the hailstorm slowed and ceased, Lemminkäinen whispered, "Beautiful horse, allow me to replace your lost fire with these glittering jewels. Allow me to place this silver bridle around your neck, and I promise I will treat you gently, I will never strike you and we will travel together on many quests."

The Fire Horse of Hiisi looked at the gems, which sparkled almost as brightly as his lost fire. He listened to the man's kind and gentle promises. So he put his head in the jewelled bridle, and let Lemminkäinen leap onto his back and guide him towards the house of Louhi.

As they trotted from the meadow, the clouds drifted away and the sun came out.

The horse's mane and tail began to dry.

The sun shone on the bridle, but the jewels were dull compared to the sparks and flames that started to smoulder along the horse's mane.

The horse was delighted to have his fire back, so he bucked and reared and danced on his hot hooves.

Lemminkäinen knew he couldn't sit on this horse for long, now the fire was burning again, so he yelled, "Gallop straight ahead, horse, get me to Louhi's house!"

But the horse gambolled and pirouetted, letting the fire from his mane trail in circles, burning Lemminkäinen's hands.

The hero gritted his teeth and ordered, "Horse, gallop to the house of Louhi."

But the Fire Horse of Hiisi was happy with

his returning flames and he ignored the man on his back.

So Lemminkäinen hit the Fire Horse of Hiisi.

The hero struck the horse with a willow stick. He kicked the horse. He shouted harsh words.

The hero had broken his promise. He hadn't treated the horse of fire gently.

The horse stopped. The horse stood still.

Then the horse of fire took a deep breath, so the flames burned faster and higher all over his body. The silver on the bridle melted. The leather burned. The jewels dropped to the ground. The willow stick turned to ash. And the flames scorched the man on his back.

Lemminkäinen screamed and leapt off the horse of fire.

The Fire Horse of Hiisi galloped back to the meadows, sparks trailing behind him.

Lemminkäinen limped back to the house of Louhi and asked for a different task to win her daughter. This new quest took him to a river, where he hunted for a swan and found his own death instead.

But the Fire Horse of Hiisi still gallops

around the meadows, his mane a waterfall of fire, his hoofprints burning into the earth. He is wild and free and happy. And he will never again believe the promises of men.

Flint Feet
Navajo myth

Once there was a time when there were no horses.

When the first horse was created, she couldn't stand. She had the long legs and the strong back of the horses that would come, but she couldn't stand on her feet.

The first people found the new horse lying on the ground, gazing at the grass but not able to reach it, gazing at the plains but not able to run on them.

The people lifted the horse onto her feet, but her feet were small and soft and weak and couldn't hold her weight. The people decided to find better feet for the horse, so she could become the fast-running, beautiful beast that her legs promised.

The first people discussed the best material for strong feet. They decided that hard sharp flint stones would work.

They saw the caterpillar crawling past and called to him, "We want to help this new creature, by giving her the feet she needs to run and jump. Can you go to the hills and fetch four flints?"

The caterpillar said, "I'd like to help, but I won't get there and back very fast crawling on the ground." The caterpillar looked longingly from the earth up to the sky. "I'd be more help to you if I had wings."

So the first people sang a song over the caterpillar and the caterpillar changed into a butterfly, with wings to carry him fast over the grass to the hills.

The butterfly flew away and returned with four grey flints. The people placed the stones gently on the soft ends of the first horse's legs.

Now the horse had hooves, and she walked and trotted and cantered and galloped, and she reared and bucked and jumped, and she kicked her hooves up in joy. And she let the first people ride her, because they had given her hooves.

And that is why the hoofprint of an unshod horse looks like the wing of a butterfly, so we remember who brought the first horse her hooves.

Bradamante and the Hippogriff

European legend

More than a thousand years ago, the Emperor Charlemagne ruled most of Europe. The emperor chose the fastest riders, the strongest warriors, the most honourable and skilled knights, to be his champions. One of his most valued champions was the Lady Bradamante.

One day Bradamante was galloping through the forest, on a white charger, with a white shield and a white plume on her helmet, on a mission for her emperor.

She met a knight galloping the other way on a mission for his prince.

The two knights circled each other and drew their swords. But the knights' horses were slowing, their heads hanging.

Bradamante said, "I think our horses are tired."

The other knight said, "Perhaps they need a rest."

So both knights agreed they would let their horses rest before duelling. They dismounted, they loosened their horses' girths, they unbuckled their swords and laid them aside, then they sat down against a wide tree trunk.

The young knight introduced himself as Rogero, and Bradamante introduced herself. They shared bread and wine, and they chatted. And though her emperor and his prince were at war, they both realised they could be friends. Possibly even more than friends. So they decided not to test their blades against each other.

But they had their missions to accomplish, so once their horses were rested, Bradamante and Rogero galloped away from each other.

A few weeks later, Bradamante heard a rumour that an enchanter on a winged horse was kidnapping knights. The next day, she heard a ballad about a magician mounted on a giant eagle, who was stealing noblemen. She didn't pay much attention, until she heard a squire whisper that a wizard on a flying monster had attacked and captured the Moorish knight Rogero.

That evening, Bradamante asked Charlemagne for a leave of absence to discover whether these rumours of a magician using a winged creature to steal knights were true and, if so, to rescue the knights.

The emperor granted her leave to free these captives in his name.

So Bradamante galloped away from the army on her white horse, towards the source of the stories, the mountainous land where most of the disappearances were reported. She stopped in the nearest town, stabled her horse and listened to the rumours, ballads, gossip and stories in the local marketplace.

Soon she'd heard enough to piece together a few facts:

There was a doorless castle high in the mountains, built on a pinnacle of rock so it wasn't accessible to anyone except its owner on his winged steed.

No one could agree what the winged steed was. A horse, or a bird, or some kind of monster?

But they did agree that the magician who had built the castle was filling it with captive knights. And he defeated the knights with a magical shield, polished so bright that when he removed its silk wrapper, an uncanny light blinded his opponents and they fell to the ground, helpless.

As she listened to the stories, Bradamante wondered how she could possibly defeat a magician with a magical shield, and how she could rescue Rogero from a castle with no way in.

Then she noticed someone else listening to the stories. A small man, in a purple silk robe, with a long curling beard.

The small man laughed at the storytellers. "Magic can only be defeated by magic. So I, Brunello, am the only one who can defeat the enchanter. I have been sent on this rescue mission by the Moorish prince himself, and the magic ring I will use to defeat the enchanter was the prince's gift to me. Every knight I rescue will owe their life to the Moorish prince, so they will give him their loyalty, they will fight for him and bring him victory.

"I will therefore defeat this enchanter *and* Charlemagne in one act."

Brunello strode out of the marketplace. Bradamante called after him, "I will accompany you into the mountains and help rescue these brave knights."

She didn't really want to help Brunello. She didn't want a whole castle of knights owing loyalty to her emperor's enemy. Also, she wanted Rogero to owe loyalty to her and to her emperor, then she and Rogero wouldn't have to fight on opposite sides.

But it wouldn't be honourable for a chivalrous knight like Bradamante to attack this small, unarmed man, so she walked beside him, chatting politely.

Suddenly Brunello said, "Look! In that cave down there, at the bottom of this cliff, there's a damsel in distress!"

Bradamante said, "I don't see anyone."

Brunello said, "She was dragged into the cave by some monster or ruffian. Don't you hear her weeping?"

Bradamante could hear a soft sighing, which might be the trees or might not. She said, "If there may be a girl in trouble, we must help her."

So Bradamante chopped down a tall slim tree with her sword, dangled it over the edge of the cliff and asked Brunello to hold the end as she climbed down.

When she was halfway down, the man in purple laughed. "I won't let anyone share my glory when I rescue these knights!"

He let go, and the tree and Bradamante plummeted to the bottom of the cliff. She fell through the air to the hard rocks beneath.

But the branches and twigs broke Bradamante's fall, she clambered back up the cliff and chased after Brunello. She could quite honourably attack him now, after he'd betrayed her and tried to kill her.

So she crept up behind him and grabbed him, winding his long beard round his neck until he was choking for breath, then she tugged the ring off his finger and hid it in her belt.

She climbed up the mountain, towards the castle. When she couldn't go any further without wings, she shouted, "Enchanter! I challenge you in the name of Charlemagne, for the life and freedom of the knight Rogero and all your other captives."

A small speck emerged from the top window of the tallest tower of the impenetrable castle.

As the shape flew nearer, Bradamante saw that the mysterious creature was both a horse and a bird. It had the body and legs of a horse, but the head and wings of an eagle.

It was a hippogriff, gleaming copper and bronze in the sun.

A man in a starry cloak sat on the hippogriff's back, holding a long staff and an oval shield covered in a black cloth.

As they flew lower, Bradamante raised her sword and slashed at the hippogriff and the enchanter.

The hippogriff swooped and swerved and kept just out of her reach. Bradamante had never fought a duel against a winged opponent before. The enemy stayed above her, moving up and down and round, and none of her blows reached their target.But the enchanter could lean down to strike Bradamante's head and shoulders with his staff.

Bradamante knew she couldn't defeat this flying horse and rider while they were in the air. However, she kept leaping and slashing and stabbing, because she wanted the enchanter to keep attacking her.

Eventually the enchanter laughed. "Let's finish this fight!" He jerked the cloth off the shield. Bradamante smiled and slipped the ring onto her finger. A strong white light blazed from the shield, but the ring dimmed Bradamante's eyes, so she could bear the violence and power of the light.

Bradamante pretended she had no magical protection. She moaned, dropped her sword, put her hands over her eyes and fell to the ground.

The enchanter clicked his tongue and the hippogriff landed. Then the enchanter flicked the black cloth over the shield and climbed down from the hippogriff. He walked towards Bradamante's still body, unwinding the rope he intended to tie her up with.

Bradamante leapt to her feet and knocked the enchanter to the ground with one punch, then tied him up with his own rope.

She removed the ring, climbed onto the hippogriff and pulled the enchanter up behind her. They flew up to the tallest tower, where Bradamante entered the impregnable castle and freed every knight held captive there.

Including Rogero.

And Rogero was so grateful to Bradamante, and to the emperor in whose name she had challenged and defeated the enchanter, that he never fought for the Moorish prince again.

In the years that followed, between battles, tournaments, jousts and duels, Bradamante and Rogero flew off on many adventures, on the back of her shining hippogriff.

And after he wriggled out of the rope, the enchanter spent the rest of his life trying to grow magical wings, so he could escape from his own castle.

The Unicorns and the Flood
Ukrainian folktale

Once upon a time, unicorns lived openly in our fields and forests. They were beautiful beasts, with cream bodies, white manes, silver horns and pearly hooves. And unicorns knew they were beautiful. They spent a lot of time gazing in still pools to admire their own reflections.

Then came the flood.

Just before the flood was due, Noah built the ark. When it was finished, Noah sent out word that he would take two of every animal on the ark to keep them safe, so they could rebuild their families, herds, flocks and colonies when dry land reappeared.

The lion and the lioness were the first to arrive. Followed by two elephants, two raccoons, two wild boars, a couple of turkeys and a pair of foxes.

Then two unicorns arrived.

"We received your invitation," the male unicorn said to Noah, at the bottom of the gangplank leading up to the ark. "It's on plain parchment, rather than the gold-edged scroll we're accustomed to, but nevertheless we thought we'd investigate what you're offering, in terms of accommodation and entertainment."

"It's an ark," said Noah. "It's waterproof and it floats. That's all I'm offering."

"Do you have first-class cabins?" asked the female unicorn.

"There aren't any private cabins, just stalls, perches and bare floor. I've got to fit in a lot of animals and birds, so everyone gets equal treatment."

The male unicorn snorted. "I'm not accustomed to equal treatment and neither is my wife. We are accustomed to being special and pampered. We don't want to live with the muck, stench and clamour of all these other animals. So I think we shall say no this time."

"There won't be another time," said Noah. "There won't be another boat. There's a flood coming and this ark is the only way to stay safe."

The female unicorn said, "But you're filling your ark with snakes, rats and spiders. Why would you do that? Why not just save the pretty animals and the ones that sing nicely? I can understand why you'd want to save the chinchilla, the peacock and the nightingale. But why save the midgie, the warthog and the skunk?"

"Because this ark is for everyone. And you are welcome, unicorns, but only if you're prepared to share."

"No," said the male unicorn. "We are not prepared to share with slugs, cockroaches and toads."

The female unicorn nodded. "We can swim. We both do a rather elegant butterfly stroke. We'll take our chances in the water, rather than lower our standards on your ark."

Noah said, "I'm sorry to hear that. And I sincerely hope you're strong swimmers."

The unicorns trotted off. They sheltered under a tree when the rain started, then paddled and swam when the waters rose.

They kept their spirits up by congratulating each other on their sensible decision to keep their distance from the crowded ark, and by chatting about the nice clean shiny world that would emerge when the flood drained away.

After a few days of swimming, they were too tired to talk, but they kept their heads and horns above water.

The rain kept falling, the floods rose higher, and the unicorns were almost too tired to swim.

Finally, the rains stopped and the sun shone on their silver horns.

The unicorns could see the ark in the distance. They could *smell* the ark in the distance. They could hear arguments and roars, snaps and growls.

They laughed, weakly. "No one is happy on that beastly boat!"

Then they saw birds fly up from the ark, sent out to find land.

Two seagulls soared in circles high above. When they spotted silver glinting in the sunlight, they swooped down and landed on the unicorns' horns.

The weight of the birds was just enough to push the hungry exhausted unicorns under the water...

Then the seagulls flew away, to look for land elsewhere.

Most storytellers say that the unicorns never floated back up, and that's why there have been no scientifically proven sightings of unicorns for a very long time.

But a few, more optimistic, storytellers say that the unicorns bobbed back up again, coughing and spluttering, then doggy-paddled to a small remote island. They say that a herd of unicorns have been happy on the island ever since, admiring themselves in pools and keeping well away from the smelly noisy crowds of animals and people everywhere else.

Which ending would you prefer to believe?

The Headless Horseman of New South Wales
Australian folktale

The butcher grinned at the tourists. "These are legendary steaks. This beef comes from the haunted riverlands, where the headless horseman roams, still screaming and moaning. Still regretting the night he stole a few cattle, was chased by the drovers and drowned in the river... Look, you can see his statue in the town square. We've been telling tales about that ghost and his trotting grey mare for years. So these are steaks with a story. Worth every cent."

The tourists smiled and paid for the steaks. Then they left the shop and took photos of themselves by the statue of the town's ghostly headless horseman.

The girl said, "Let's camp by that haunted river tonight!"

The boy said, "But what if the ghost tries to steal us?"

The mum said, "This ghost only steals cattle."

The dad said, "Anyway, there's no such thing as ghosts."

So they decided to camp near the haunted river.

The tourists followed the map, pitched their tent, lit their barbecue, cooked their legendary steaks and enjoyed the beauty of the wide starry sky.

They fell asleep, full and happy.

Just after midnight, they were woken by a scream. A wailing, ululating, terrifying scream. When the scream died away, they heard thundering hoofbeats. They peered out of the tent and saw a figure galloping past on a dark grey horse.

The horse was strong and fast, her head and neck stretched out as she galloped. The man on her back was tall and bulky. His hands gripped the horse's reins. His legs gripped the horse's ribs. But he had no head. His long cloaked back ended in square shoulders and the stub of a neck.

He had no head.

It was the headless horseman!

The family screamed, scrambled into their car, locked the doors and argued in panicked whispers about whose fault it was they'd camped by a haunted river.

Five minutes later, the horseman trotted past in the other direction, driving two cows in front of him.

The tourists heard the horse neighing, the cows mooing and the headless horseman laughing.

The girl whispered, "How can he laugh when he has *no head*?"

But the headless horseman was still laughing when he drove the stolen cows into the shed at the back of the butcher's shop. He lifted off the cloth-covered frame that hid his head and gave him a long back. Then he unsaddled his grey mare and got ready to restock his shelves for the next day.

In the morning, the butcher grinned at a new family of tourists. "These are legendary steaks. This beef comes from the haunted riverlands..." The tourists smiled and got out their wallets.

The Kelpie with the Tangled Mane

Scottish folktale

The shore of a loch, like the forest edge or the seaside, is a place where worlds meet. It can be a dangerous place to live and work.

But Meg was used to living on the lochside, and knew she had to be careful of the creatures that prowled the border between land and water.

Her family had farmed the land by the water for generations. Their days were filled with hard work and their nights were filled with stories of the creatures that lived in the loch.

Meg's father told stories about the kelpies, who were monsters underwater, but became elegant horses or handsome people on the land, luring girls and boys into the loch to drown them and eat them.

And her grandmother told stories of giant eels, talking salmon and the ancient goddess of the water, though no one had seen her for a very long time.

Everyone had seen the other creatures that lived in the loch. The magical water bulls didn't eat people, but they were still fierce and dangerous. The water bulls sometimes came ashore to meet and mate with the farmer's cattle, and their calves were always hungry eaters with odd notches in their ears. But the water bulls' calves were also strong and healthy, so they were prized.

One summer a water bull lingered too long in their fields. Meg's father offered hay to the water bull and when the animal lowered his head to eat, the farmer slipped a halter around his neck, then locked him in a barn. Meg's father was considering taking the bull to market, to see if he could get a good price for this magical creature.

Meg hoped her father would either sell the bull soon or release him, because she could hear the water bull's angry roars and sad bellows wherever she worked on the farm.

Then, one sunny afternoon, Meg finished her day's work early and had a few moments to herself before it was time to make supper. She sat by the loch, looking at the silver ripples on the water.

A voice said, "It's beautiful, isn't it?"

Meg looked up and saw a handsome young man, with wild blond hair and a slow smile.

"I love to look at the loch," she said, "but I know never to go in."

"The water is beautiful, but it's not as lovely as you," he said with a wider smile.

Meg blushed, and couldn't think of a sensible reply.

"May I sit beside you?" he asked.

She nodded.

They sat together and watched the light slide across the loch.

The young man asked Meg if she had a comb.

"Yes, in my apron pocket."

"Would you mind combing my hair? It gets tangled on a day wandering the hills."

Meg nodded and he laid his head in her lap. She started to untangle his long golden hair. In the warm afternoon sun, with her fingers gentle on his scalp, the young man dozed off.

As she combed, Meg found strands of waterweed in the man's hair.

Waterweed? But he said he'd spent the day wandering the hills. How could he have waterweed in his hair?

Then she remembered those night-time stories about the creatures from the loch. The stories about the kelpies, who could become elegant horses to lure you into the water, but could also disguise themselves as handsome people.

Was she sitting on the lochside with a kelpie?

Meg looked at the young man's clothes. Everything he wore was rich and fine, but all the fabrics were green and blue, the colours of the loch in the sunlight. His buttons were silver like the ripples on the water. And his hair was softly waving in the breeze, like waterweed under the surface.

She *was* sitting on the lochside with a kelpie…

How could she get away, without waking him?

Meg untied her apron and slid herself out from under the sleeping kelpie, pillowing his head on the apron and the grass beneath.

She started to creep towards the farm. After a dozen slow, soft, scared steps, she looked behind her.

The young man was yawning and stretching. He was waking up!

Meg stopped walking slowly and softly. She started to run as fast as she could in her long skirts and heavy boots.

She heard a yell of anger behind her. Then she heard hoofbeats.

She glanced over her shoulder, and she saw a huge pale stallion with a long golden mane, one section smooth and combed, the rest all tangled with waterweed.

The massive stallion was galloping straight towards her.

Meg picked up her skirts and sprinted.

But the horse was much faster, so fast that she could already feel his hot breath on her neck.

She was still a long way from the safety of the farmhouse. But she was almost at the barn where the water bull was locked up.

Then the horse caught her.

Meg felt teeth biting at the back of her dress. She turned to the side, out from under those hooves, and jerked away. She felt the collar of her dress rip.

She rolled to the ground and hauled herself up on the latch of the barn door. Then she dragged the door open and leapt out of the way.

The furious water bull burst out of his prison and collided with the furious kelpie.

Meg sheltered behind the wall of the barn as the two water beasts fought. The kelpie fought with his speed and his hooves; the bull fought with his weight and his horns.

They kicked and bit, gouged and gored, wrestled and charged, screamed and roared. The kelpie's rage at losing his prey and the water bull's rage at being imprisoned fuelled a vicious fight.

The two angry water beasts battled each other right to the edge of the loch. Meg watched as they both toppled into the water and, with one great splash, the horse and the bull were gone.

Neither of them was ever seen again on the shores of that loch.

So Meg's father never took a water bull to market.

And Meg had her own tale to tell about the creatures of the loch, when her family shared stories in the dark of the night.

The Wise Colt
Jewish folktale

There was once a father with twelve sons, who also owned a beautiful mare with twelve foals. So he allowed his twelve sons, in order of their birth, to choose a horse each. The youngest son was left with the smallest colt.

The smallest colt was skinny, scabby, bald in patches, knock-kneed and a bit smelly.

His brothers laughed at the youngest son and his pathetic colt, but the boy smiled at the horse. "Don't mind them. I'll look after you."

The horse whispered back, "And I'll look after you."

The boy jumped in surprise, but the colt spoke again. "If you take me into the woods, I'll guide you to a magical waterfall where I can wash, then I won't be such an embarrassment to you."

So the boy rode the colt to the waterfall, where the bony patchy horse stood under the rushing water, and was washed clean and healthy. When he was dry, the boy brushed and combed him. Now the colt's flanks were spotless and clear, his mane was long and glistening, his legs were strong and perfect, his neck was arched and he was the most beautiful and fragrant horse in the world.

After that the boy took the colt's advice on everything.

Until one day the boy saw a long shape gleaming in the grass in front of his horse's hooves. He leapt off the horse's back and picked up a golden feather, shining with the warmth and beauty of a summer's day.

The colt said, "Put that down."

The boy said, "But it's so beautiful."

"It is beautiful, but it's also trouble. That

golden feather will bring you worry and fear and pain. Put it down."

The boy shook his head. "If I put it down, it might be lost forever. Any object this precious and beautiful should be treasured, and kept among other splendid objects."

So the boy held the feather carefully as he rode the colt to the king's palace, where he offered the golden feather as a gift to the king.

The king was so impressed with the gift that he made the boy his cupbearer.

That evening, the boy groomed his colt in the royal stables. "Now my brothers won't laugh at me or at you! So that feather has brought me luck, not pain and worry."

But the former cupbearer, who had lost his job so the king could favour the boy, was angry and jealous. He crept up behind the throne and whispered in the king's ear that a boy who had one golden feather would probably have the whole golden bird. "He must be keeping the bird for himself, rather than giving it to you, like any true loyal subject would."

The king summoned the boy to the foot of his throne. "I want the bird that feather came from. Either you have the bird yourself or you know where it is. Fetch the golden bird for me or I will cut off your head."

The boy said that he'd found the feather lying on the ground and he'd never seen the golden bird.

The king shrugged. "You found a golden feather, you can find a golden bird. Bring me the bird or lose your head."

The boy ran to the stables and told the colt about the king's demand. "You were right, that feather is causing me worry and fear, and I suppose there will be pain too, briefly, if he cuts my head off. I'm sorry I didn't follow your advice, wise colt."

"If you follow my advice now, we might be able to save you."

"Do you know where the bird is?"

"I know where it can be found. Bring a net." The boy found a net and they galloped out of the palace.

The colt carried the boy over fields and

hills to a walled garden. "There are hundreds of apple trees in there, but the bird roosts in the same tree each night. Search the orchard for the tree with feathers under it. Pick up one of the feathers, climb the tree, wait for the bird to settle down to sleep, then capture it."

The boy nodded and entered the walled garden.

Inside the walls, the scent of ripe apples was sweet and warm. He searched under the branches of all the trees and in the very centre of the orchard he found a scattering of golden feathers. He put one in his pocket and climbed the nearest tree.

By the time he reached the highest branches that would hold his weight, his fingers were grazed and bleeding. "I hope that's the most pain these golden feathers cause me," he whispered, as he perched uncomfortably on a branch.

He waited and waited.

As the sun sank below the top of the high wall, leaving streaks of colour behind it, the boy heard the most beautiful sound. A high, long, swooping song. He sat in the tree, gazing at the pink and orange sky, smelling the sweet apples, listening to the entrancing song. He felt tears run down his cheeks.

Then the bright golden-feathered bird landed on a branch, sang its last verse, tucked its golden head under its golden wing and fell asleep.

The boy looked at the bird, free to fly among the clouds, sing in the open air and roost high in the trees. He thought of the king's palace, with its stone walls and echoing corridors. He didn't want to capture the bird.

He didn't want to lose his head either.

So he threw the net over the bird and bundled it under his arm. He tried to soothe its panicked struggles with gentle words, as he climbed back down the apple tree and returned to his wise colt outside the walls.

They rode back to the palace, in silence.

The king thanked the boy for the golden bird and locked it in an iron cage. But the displaced cupbearer whispered, "The bird is beautiful, but surely it came from a golden cage. Probably that new boy has kept the valuable cage for himself, rather than giving it to you, like any true loyal subject would."

The king summoned the boy to the foot of his throne. "I want the golden cage that bird came from. Either you have the cage yourself or you know where it is. Fetch the golden cage for me or I will cut off your head."

The boy said that he'd caught the bird sitting in a tree, in the open, after hearing its song, and that he had never seen the bird in a cage.

The king shrugged. "You found a golden bird, you can find a golden cage. Bring me the cage or lose your head."

The boy ran to the stables to tell the wise colt about the king's new demand. "You were right, that feather is still causing me worry and trouble. I'm sorry I didn't follow your advice."

"If you follow my advice now, we might be able to save you."

"Do you know where the golden cage is?"

"I know where it can be found. Bring the feather you picked up in the orchard."

The colt carried the boy over fields and hills to a dark castle. "Enter the castle and you will find rooms full of golden objects. Do not touch any of them or you will be turned to gold yourself. In the last room you will find a golden cage. Put the bird's feather inside the cage, then it will be safe for you to lift the cage and take it to your demanding king."

The boy entered the windowless castle and pulled the golden feather from his pocket. The feather lit the darkness, and he saw golden tables, golden chairs, golden apples, golden tapestries, golden suits of armour, golden dogs, golden swords, golden men and golden women. He remembered the advice of his wise colt and he didn't touch anything.

He walked through the cold glittering castle until he reached a room with only one object. An intricate golden cage, with a perch inside for a bird and curving sides of woven gold wire.

It was beautiful, but it was a prison.

He dropped the feather inside and the feather dimmed. He picked the cage up and ran back through the castle to his wise colt outside the door.

They rode quietly back to the palace.

"Here, Your Majesty, is a golden cage fit for the golden bird."

The king thanked him, and had the bird removed from the iron cage and put in the golden cage. The bird sat on the perch, silent and still.

The former cupbearer whispered in the king's ear, "Why does the bird not sing for you? That new boy controls the bird, and he won't let it sing for you, like any true loyal subject would."

The king summoned the boy to the foot of his throne. "Make the bird sing for me. You told me about its beautiful song, I want to hear it. So make the bird sing or I will cut off your head."

The boy sighed. He looked at the bird, hunched and silent in the cage. He didn't need to ask the wise colt for advice this time, because he knew what he had to do, even it if cost him his head.

He said to the king, "The bird does not sing, because the bird is sad. The bird is trapped in a cage in a palace, rather than flying free in the wind and clouds. If you want to hear the golden bird's beautiful song, allow me to let it go."

The king looked at the bird, then at the boy, and he nodded.

The boy opened the cage. The bird flew out and circled the throne room, singing its sweet, swooping song. Everyone in the palace started to sob, as they heard the beauty of the song.

Then the golden bird fluttered out of a high window and flew away, forever.

After hearing the song, the king sent the ex-cupbearer away and kept the boy by his side as his trusted advisor. When he grew old, the king named the boy his heir.

When the boy became king in his turn, he always listened to the advice of his wise horse. Though he never entirely regretted ignoring the colt's advice on the day he found the golden feather...

Fire and Clay
Indian tribal tale

The creator made the first woman and the first man out of clay. As they dried in the sun, all the first animals came to look at them.

The first horse, a fiery stallion with flaming wings, saw that future men and women would work horses hard. Horses without fire or wings would be forced to gallop far and fast, pull heavy weights and fight in dangerous battles. The first horse wanted to protect his grandchildren from the hard work ahead.

So he rose into the air on his burning wings

and he kicked the two clay figures to dust, which floated away on the wind.

The horse snorted and galloped off.

The creator thought the world wasn't complete without people. So the creator decided to make another pair of clay figures. But before moulding them, the creator made the first spider and whispered to the spider what her first job would be.

Once the creator had made the clay woman and clay man, the spider wound strong silvery cobwebs around them.

When the fiery first horse came galloping past again, and saw two more figures threatening a future of work and danger, he kicked out at the new clay man and the new clay woman. But the spider's web held the drying clay together and the figures stayed solid and firm.

Soon the flaming stallion gave up. He wasn't keen on hard work for himself either.

When the figures were dry, the creator breathed life into them. And those two clay people became our first grandmother and our first grandfather.

And they did work horses hard, to build this world for us.

So that is how the first horse tried to destroy us, and how the first spider protected us.

And that is why we should always be grateful to spiders.

Selling the Goddess
Tibetan tale

Goodheart was a kind and generous young man, who was always in trouble with his rich father for giving money *to* the poor, rather than making money *from* them. So Goodheart left home and wandered the world, accepting charity from strangers when he had nothing, and giving generously to strangers when he had something.

One evening, he lay down to sleep under a tall pine tree on the edge of a great green forest.

In the night, he heard the tree sigh and felt the trunk shiver. In the starlight, he saw a tall slim woman step down the tree from the highest twigs to the lowest branches, as if she was walking down a staircase. The young woman jumped to the ground and sat beside him.

She was wearing a long green dress, with a green silk scarf over her long black hair. She smiled at Goodheart and asked what he was doing in the forest with no horse, no pack, no money and no food.

He told her about his arguments with his father, and his wanderings. She told him about her life, as goddess of the trees in the forest.

After they'd chatted most of the night, the goddess said, "I've seen many men pass through the forest, but none of them have been as kind and generous and goodhearted as you."

He sighed. "My family didn't approve of my generosity."

The goddess shrugged. "I have a difficult family too. But you are the kindest and best man I've ever seen, so I wonder... would you consider… do you think…?" But the goddess didn't reach the end of her question before the sun came up.

As the sun rose, a small bush trotted towards them and said, "My Lady, your father wants to see this young man and set him a task."

The goddess of the trees frowned. "My father is the giant of the forest. He wants to test you, to see if you're worthy of being my husband."

Goodheart blushed. "Your husband?"

She nodded. "If you'd like to marry me, you'll have to complete this task. But I'll understand if you don't want to. My dad is quite scary."

"Oh yes, I'd be happy to. If you'd like me to, that is." Goodheart was blushing even more.

The goddess smiled. "I would very much like you to. But to complete the task you'll need this." She slid a sharp bronze axe from her sleeve. "He'll ask you to chop wood, because that's how he judges a man, and this axe will help you."

So Goodheart followed the bush to the

centre of the forest, where a huge bristly green giant asked him to chop three piles of wood with three blows of the axe.

The piles of wood were as high as Goodheart's head, but he lifted the axe and brought it down – one, two, three times – and the axe sliced each pile into little sticks of kindling. Then he put the axe down.

The giant laughed. "You are indeed worthy of my precious girl. But her mother won't be so easy to persuade."

The goddess appeared beyond the heaps of kindling. "My mother, the witch of the forest, has also summoned you. I'll take you to her cave."

As they walked, the goddess slid another blade from her sleeve. A bright silver dagger. "My mother can be frightening. Hold this blade between you and her at all times. And if necessary, use it fast to defend yourself."

Goodheart's hand trembled as he took the dagger. Then he stepped into the cave.

In the shadowy corner was a hunched figure. "I hear you want to marry my daughter."

"Yes, I do. And she wants to marry me."

"What can you offer her?"

Goodheart held the blade casually in front of him, as he considered his answer. "Um. A good heart, I suppose. And willing hands to build a life for us both."

"Can you offer her kingdoms and empires, riches and power?"

"No, not really. But I don't think she wants that."

"I want it, for her!" The figure in the corner leapt at him, changing in mid-air into a grey serpent with a tongue of flame.

Without thinking, Goodheart lifted the blade. As the snake struck at his face, the dagger pierced her throat.

And the goddess's mother fell to the cave floor.

Her tongue of flame flickered out.

The witch was dead.

Goodheart was horrified. He walked slowly out of the cave and said to the goddess, "I'm so sorry, my dear, I've done something terrible."

The goddess glanced into the cave, then turned away, her face pale. "My poor mother. And my poor Goodheart. I'm sorry she attacked you. It was her nature. She has killed and eaten most of my friends. That's why I gave you the dagger. But my father will be angry. We must leave the forest right now."

They started to run, but the ground behind them was already shaking. The giant was chasing them, with an army of green leafy warriors.

The goddess said to Goodheart, "This is not your fault. This is not your family. I should never have involved you. Run and save yourself, my Goodheart. I'll try to stop my father. If I succeed, I'll follow you."

She gave him a quick kiss, slid a long golden sword from her sleeve and turned to face her father.

Goodheart lifted the dagger. "I will fight beside you."

She laughed. "You have a good strong heart, but you're not a warrior. If you love me, then run from the forest and keep running. Now!"

So he ran. And he kept running.

Behind him, the goddess fought. She fought on foot and cut down hundreds of leafy warriors with her long golden sword. Then she rose on a white cloud into the air and cut down hundreds more.

Her father whirled the sharp bronze axe. But the blade didn't come close to the goddess, because she was nimble and she swung her sword faster than a lumbering giant could swing an axe.

Finally, the giant stood still among the shredded leaves and broken twigs of all his warriors.

The goddess said, "I'm sorry about the witch. But she did attack first. Now I'm going to leave the forest and be with my Goodheart. Could we have your blessing?"

Her father screamed, "No!" and threw the axe at her. It broke the blade of her sword and she tumbled off the cloud. As the goddess fell, she turned into a white horse. Then she galloped away faster than the giant could run.

The white horse galloped far from the forest

and eventually caught up with Goodheart. The white horse slowed down so that she could trot beside Goodheart as he ran.

Goodheart said, "What a splendid horse. Though I wasn't hoping for a horse, I was hoping for my beautiful, wise, brave goddess of the trees. So I won't ride you, lovely horse, in case we go too fast for her to catch up." He turned to look at the forest in the distance. "Perhaps I've already been running too fast. I should slow down now, and hope she reaches me soon."

The horse nuzzled his shoulder. Goodheart said, "We'd better find you something to eat."

He led the horse to the next village and asked politely for hay and apples for his friend the white horse. Then he found her a warm stable, while he slept on the ground.

The next morning, he looked back at the empty road from the forest and sighed. "Perhaps I've lost her forever…"

The horse nuzzled him again, but Goodheart kept gazing at the forest.

They walked to the next town, where a

magician saw the white horse, and thought there was something magical about her. "Is this horse for sale?" he asked Goodheart.

Goodheart replied, "I don't have the money to keep a splendid horse like this as she deserves, so if you promise to be kind to her, I will sell her for the price of a bed, a bath and a hot meal."

The horse whinnied and stamped on the ground.

The magician quickly threw three gold coins at Goodheart and took the white horse away.

Goodheart left the town and kept walking slowly away from the forest.

The magician led the white horse to his house. "Let's see what you really are," he said, as he pushed her deep into the flames of a large bread oven.

Before the magician could close the door, the horse changed into a tiny white bird and darted out of the oven.

The magician chased the bird, who changed into a white cloud, floated into the sky and floated away from the town.

Then the cloud hovered above Goodheart and rained heavily on his head.

The goddess changed back to her human form and stood in front of him, with her arms crossed.

"My darling, you survived!" He gave her a hug.

"I survived," she said. "And then you sold me! For three gold coins!"

Goodheart said, "Oh! Were you the splendid white horse? I'm sorry, I didn't recognise you."

The goddess smiled. "Now you've seen me as a tree, and a woman, and a horse. I was the cloud who rained on you too. You've seen me unable to change out of my horse form, after using up so much energy in battle, until I drew extra power from a fire. And you've met my father the giant and my mother the witch. Do you still want to marry me?"

"Of course! But you've seen me run away, and fail to recognise you, and sell you to a magician. Do you still want to marry me?"

"Of course!"

So Goodheart and the goddess were married. They used the three gold coins to set up in business as woodcarvers, carving beautiful pictures of trees, clouds and horses. Whenever they had more than enough money for themselves and their growing family, they gave the extra coins away. Because Goodheart still had a good heart...

The Centaur's Heroes
Greek myth

Centaurs love parties. They particularly love crashing other people's parties, where they use their horse hooves to dance on the tables, and their human heads to sing rude songs and to chant their catchphrase: "Half horse, half man, ALL party animal!"

But one centaur was different. Chiron thought partying every day and every night was a waste of time, and he didn't think it was fair to wreck people's wedding parties, birthday parties and house-warming parties.

So Chiron studied. He read ancient books, mapped the stars, played the harp and learnt about herbs.

Chiron became a scholar and a healer. He moved away from his centaur herd in the valley and set up a school in the mountains. He hoped to train centaur foals to be less rowdy and more responsible; he hoped to build a herd of educated and heroic centaurs.

All the other centaurs laughed at him. They weren't interested in books or plants or stars or science. They just wanted to know where the next birthday cake was coming from and who was paying for the lemonade.

So Chiron invited human children to his school. He gave them space and encouragement to learn weapon skills in practice bouts against each other, and he taught them ethics, healing, philosophy, music, algebra, politeness and leadership skills.

Over the years, Chiron trained many of the greatest Greek heroes, including Jason, who found the Golden Fleece; Achilles and Ajax, who fought at Troy; Asclepius, who became a famous healer; and the fearsome monster-killers Theseus, Perseus and Hercules.

But Chiron never lost his desire to train a centaur hero. So, one day, he trotted down the mountain to visit his old herd, to see if there were any young centaurs interested in astronomy, philosophy and mathematics.

He reached his home valley to find the centaur herd crashing another birthday party. The children were terrified by the huge half-men half-horses stomping about their picnic, crushing the cakes and the crisps.

The centaurs were daring each other to make the children scream even louder. The noise could be heard all over the valley and the mountains beyond.

Chiron leapt onto a picnic table, scattering fairy cakes and bowls of olives. He yelled, "Stop scaring the guests! Can't you be polite and ask for cake nicely?"

The other centaurs pointed at him, high on the table. "Look, Chiron is going to dance for us. Show us your party piece, Chiron!"

But Chiron tried to lecture them about civic responsibility and good relations with your neighbours.

The other centaurs laughed, threw slices of chocolate cake at him, then grabbed the small party guests and started chucking them around in a violent game of piggy in the middle.

Then a hero arrived.

Hercules, one of Greece's greatest heroes, heard the screams and came to investigate.

Hercules saw the centaurs causing chaos and the children in danger. So he set an arrow to his bow and considered which centaur to shoot first.

He recalled workshops on ethical warfare at his tutor Chiron's mountain school, where they discussed whether killing the leader of a band of warriors might cause the rest to retreat or surrender, resulting in a faster victory and less bloodshed.

So Hercules aimed at the centaur on the table, the centaur shouting orders, the centaur covered in chocolate and cream, the centaur the rest of the herd were pointing at.

Hercules aimed at Chiron.

Hercules let the arrow fly.

And Hercules shot his arrow right into his old tutor's chest.

Chiron fell from the table.

The other centaurs wheeled around and saw the huge heavily armed hero putting another arrow to his bowstring, so they dropped the children and bolted, galloping off across the valley.

The children ran to Hercules. "Thank you so much for saving our party. But why did you shoot the nice centaur, the one who was trying to stop the nasty scary centaurs?"

Hercules ran to the fallen centaur, wiped the cake from his face and finally recognised his old tutor.

Hercules held Chiron's head on his lap, as the centaur spoke his final words. "Thank you for saving the party guests. It's good to know that my pupils have learnt to be heroes, even if my herd aren't yet ready."

Chiron closed his eyes and took his last breath. Out of respect for all the heroes he'd trained, the gods immortalised him as a constellation of stars in the sky.

Nowadays centaurs are more careful about which parties they crash, in case Hercules is a guest. And Chiron, the best centaur of them all, is still galloping across the sky, hoping that one day he will see a heroic centaur gallop the earth below…

What You Learn at Wolf School
Balkan folktale

The young wolf had just finished his year at wolf school. He'd howled in the school choir, he'd studied reading and writing and pack etiquette and paw care and the phases of the moon, and he'd also learnt the most important rule of being a wolf:

If you don't know its name, don't eat it.

That was the rule they repeated every morning and every afternoon:

If you don't know its name, don't eat it.

Because, the wolf school pupils were told,

if you don't know an animal's name, then you don't know whether it's safe to eat. It might give you a tummy ache. It might bite back. It might even want to eat you. So:

If you don't know its name, don't eat it.

But the young wolf was hungry. (Wolves in stories are usually hungry, because full sleepy wolves aren't as exciting as hungry prowling wolves.)

The hungry young wolf was trotting through the woods, when he saw a big glossy animal, tied to a tree.

Tied to a tree! It couldn't run away! This was the very best kind of food for a young wolf, like a picnic or a packed lunch…

There was just one problem. The young wolf didn't know what this juicy-looking animal was. He didn't know its name. So he knew he shouldn't eat it.

But after a full year of wolf school, and winning top prizes in howling and paw care, this young wolf knew he was very clever, and he was sure there was a way round the *If you don't know its name, don't eat it* rule.

So the wolf trotted up to the big glossy animal tied to the tree and said, "Hello! What's your name?"

The big animal flicked her tail. "I don't know."

"Of course you do. Everyone knows their name. So, what's your name?"

The big animal tossed her mane. "I don't have a name."

"Come on," said the wolf. "Everything has a name. Look around. That's a crow, that's a worm, I'm a wolf and you are…?"

The big animal shuffled her heavy feet. "I don't know. I really don't know."

"You must have a name. Everyone is given a name."

The big animal looked sad. "No one has ever given me anything."

"Aw!" said the wolf. "Really? No one has ever given you ANYTHING?"

"Well, the farmer gave me four shoes last week." Her ears pricked up. "Maybe my name is on my shoes!"

The wolf thought about the name tags on

his gym kit at wolf school, and nodded. "Yes, your name might be on your shoes."

The big animal tossed her mane again. "Why don't you have a look? Why don't you see if you can read my name for me?"

The wolf grinned. "Why not? Then you'll know your name. And so will I!" He licked his lips.

The big animal lifted her back right foot. "See if you can read anything on this shoe."

The wolf walked round behind the animal's back legs and looked at the curve of metal on the bottom of her foot. "I see nails and scratches, but no letters."

"Perhaps you should come closer and look more carefully."

The wolf stepped closer to the back leg. "I still can't see anything."

"Try a little closer..."

"No, still nothing."

"Try even closer..."

The wolf stepped right up to the huge, heavy, iron-shod hoof.

And the big animal kicked as hard as she could.

The wolf ran off howling, "Owowowowow!" with his nose bruised and sore.

The young wolf still doesn't know the big animal's name, though he does know she's far too dangerous to eat.

But I'm sure you know what she was!

The Horse Who Fought a Lion

Persian legend

Rostam was a hero. He'd been learning how to be a hero since he was a small boy, and now he had almost everything a hero needed. He had a sword, a spear and the start of a splendid moustache. He'd even won a few victories over his king's enemies.

But he didn't have a hero's horse.

So he visited the finest herd of horses in Persia. He approached each horse, laid his right hand on the horse's back and pressed down hard. Every horse crumpled to the ground, because no horse could bear the weight of Rostam's strong fighting hand.

Then he roped the wildest, reddest, fastest horse in the herd and pressed hard on the young stallion's back. The horse stood steady and calm, no matter how hard Rostam pushed.

So the red horse was chosen to become the hero's horse. Rostam named him Rakush, which means lightning.

This is the story of Rostam and Rakush's first journey together, as hero and horse, travelling through the desert on a mission for the king of Persia.

After a tiring day crossing the sands, Rostam and Rakush stopped for the night by a small pool. Rostam fell asleep and Rakush kept watch.

But they weren't the only ones resting by the water. A lion was watching them from the shadows of the reeds.

The lion thought that a fresh crunchy hero would make a tasty supper. The lion also thought that a grass-eating saddle-wearing horse would be no match for a meat-eating wild-haired lion.

So the lion ignored Rakush and crept towards Rostam.

But Rakush was a hero's horse. When he saw the lion stalking the sleeping hero, Rakush attacked.

The horse's strong teeth tore chunks out of the lion's mane, so the lion tried to bite the horse's legs. Rakush leapt away from the teeth, so the lion stretched out his sharp claws and scratched the horse's side. Rakush reared up and kicked out with his heavy hooves, bruising the lion's ribs.

The lion roared in pain, decided that heroes probably didn't taste as good as goats anyway and ran off.

Rakush shook his mane and stood guard over Rostam again. But the lion's roars had woken the hero.

"What have you been doing, horse?" Rostam looked at the tracks on the ground and the scratches on Rakush's flanks. "Have you been fighting lions? All on your own, without waking me?"

Rakush nodded.

"That was foolish. I'm the hero! You're just my horse. What if the lion had slashed your throat rather than your side? I'd have been stuck here with a dead horse and no way of crossing the desert. So no more fighting on your own. Wake me up next time and let me do the fighting."

Rostam fell asleep again, muttering about horses who thought they were heroes.

Rakush kept watch all night, but the lion didn't come back.

The next day was dry and hot, and when the sun finally went down the hero and his horse were lost and thirsty. They couldn't find any water, until Rostam followed a wild sheep to the tiny spring of water it drank from every night.

Rather than killing the wild sheep for his supper, Rostam thanked it for leading them to water and wished it a long, happy life.

As he settled down for the night, Rostam said to the horse, "No fighting enemies on your own for fun, Rakush. If you see anything dangerous, wake me up and let me do the fighting. I'm the hero, remember. You're just the horse."

Rostam lay down and Rakush stood on guard.

Then, at the edge of the light from the campfire, Rakush saw a long curved claw. The claw moved away. He saw a massive eye, glaring at him. The eye blinked and vanished. He saw a wide nostril and a wisp of smoke.

There was a dragon, in the darkness, watching them.

Rakush had been forbidden to fight on his own. Anyway, the dragon was much bigger than the lion. So the horse stamped his hoof on the ground to wake Rostam.

Rostam leapt up like a hero, with his hand on his sword before his eyes were fully open. He looked around. But the dragon had stepped back into the deep darkness of the desert.

"Why did you wake me?" demanded Rostam.

Rakush nodded towards the darkness.

Rostam peered into the night. "I don't see anything. There's no lion there. Don't wake me again for no good reason." He went back to sleep and started to snore.

Rakush stared into the darkness. There, at the edge of the firelight, he saw a scaly tail slither.

The dragon was back!

This time the dragon stepped into the light. It was a silver dragon, with a smile wider than the horse was long. The dragon moved on clawed feet, slowly and silently, towards Rostam. Its forked tongue licked its sharp teeth.

So Rakush stamped again.

Rostam sat up and rubbed his eyes. By the time he looked round, the dragon had gone.

Rostam scowled at Rakush. "I'm not sure you're the right horse for me, after all. A hero's horse can't be afraid of the dark. A hero's horse can't be scared by shadows. And a hero needs a good night's sleep. So if you wake me up one more time, I'll find a new horse to carry me on my quests."

The hero pulled his cloak over his head and snored even more loudly.

The dragon stepped back into the light and grinned at the horse.

Rakush didn't know what to do. Rostam

had ordered him not to fight enemies on his own, so he couldn't fight the dragon. And if he woke Rostam up again, he'd lose his new job as the hero's horse.

Rakush flicked his tail and shuffled his hooves. What could he do?

The dragon crept towards Rostam, smoke rising from its nostrils, its long tongue snaking towards the hero.

Rakush decided Rostam's safety was more important than his job. So he stamped his hooves.

Rostam woke up and leapt up, but this time he aimed his sword at Rakush, as the dragon stepped backwards out of the light.

"You stupid noisy disobedient horse?" Rostam yelled. "How dare you wake me up again?"

Rakush backed away from the angry hero. Rostam followed the horse, shouting and waving his sword.

Rakush backed to the edge of the light. Then he stamped his hooves in a circle. Stamping and stamping, round and round, as Rostam yelled, "Stop making that noise and listen to what I'm shouting at you!" But Rakush kept stamping until Rostam looked down.

On the sand, framed by a circle of hoofprints, Rostam saw one huge clawed footprint.

Rostam lowered his sword and smiled at Rakush, then said clearly, "If you wake me up again, horse, I'll make horsemeat stew for breakfast. Stand still, keep quiet, remember what I said about horses not fighting, and I might let you be my horse in the morning."

Rostam winked, returned to his blanket and lay down.

Rakush watched as the dragon stepped into the light and walked confidently towards Rostam, who was making loud snoring noises.

The dragon looked at the horse. The horse shrugged, to show the dragon that he couldn't fight, he couldn't wake Rostam up, he would just have to watch as the dragon ate his hero.

The dragon leant over Rostam and slowly opened his jaws.

But Rostam leapt up, sword in one hand and spear in the other. The wide-awake hero attacked the surprised dragon.

The dragon fought with teeth and claws. The hero fought with blades and points. Sometimes the dragon flung the hero to the ground, sometimes the hero forced the dragon to back off. Sometimes they rolled out of the light, sometimes they rolled towards the fire.

Then the dragon wrapped its coils tightly around the hero, and suddenly Rostam couldn't stab with his sword or aim with his spear.

Rakush neighed. And Rostam said, "All right, you can fight if you want to."

So the horse leapt onto the dragon's back, kicking and stamping and biting.

The hero and his horse fought the dragon together. The dragon wailed and writhed, and finally lay panting on the ground at the hero's feet and the horse's hooves.

Rostam spoke sternly to the dragon, "I will let you go, if you promise not to attack travellers, or their horses, ever again."

The dragon nodded and limped out of the circle of light.

Rostam lay back down, but just before his eyes closed, he sat up.

"Why don't you sleep, Rakush?" he said. "I'll keep watch, while you have a rest. You have to carry me a long way tomorrow, you deserve sleep too."

Rakush settled down, while Rostam kept watch for lions or dragons or any other enemies he could fight, with his hero's horse by his side.

Following the Trail of Magical Horses

I grew up in a rural part of Scotland, and I did what lots of girls in rural areas do – I rode horses. I had riding lessons every Saturday, and I trotted and cantered, I jumped, I groomed, I mucked out. And I loved it.

I live in a city now and I don't spend a lot of time with horses. But I haven't lost my love for them, or my fascination with them, particularly with horses' roles in stories.

What I love about horses nowadays, as a storyteller and writer, is their beauty, but also their power. The horses and ponies I knew were all well trained, but they could still hurt you, if they kicked or even stood on you accidentally. When I was standing beside them, I was always aware of the size, weight, power and potential danger of horses. And these were horses I loved.

But imagine being a soldier on foot as a knight on horseback charged at you. Horses are beautiful, but they can also be terrifying. And I wanted to reflect that power and fear in these stories, as well as the role horses have as our companions and helpers.

These are not pony-club tales about gymkhanas. These are stories about warriors and monsters, stories about the origin of horses and the origin of people, stories in which horses can be magical, stories in which horses are not always the goodies.

This has been one of the most challenging collections of myths and legends I've ever written, because it was almost impossible to choose which fifteen stories to tell, from the thousands of amazing horse stories out there. Every human culture that grew up with horses has brilliant horse myths and legends.

Even places where horses only arrived in the last few centuries, like Australia, have lots of horse folklore.

In the end, I just chose the stories I love the best. That's why there are plenty of monster-defeating stories, and stories about the relationship between heroes and their horses, and also a centaur and a kelpie, because those are my favourite magical horses.

As I tell these stories, I change them a little (or sometimes a lot!) to make them fit my voice and the audiences I tell them to. Traditional tales have always changed to stay alive, and I'm just adding my small tweaks to the evolution of these horse stories. If you tell them to someone else, I hope you add or subtract or twist a little as well.

If you want to read the horse stories that inspired me, here are the details of where I found them:

Pegasus and the Monsters
Greek myth

I've known the Perseus and Pegasus part of this myth since I was a child, and I honestly can't recall where I first read it. (Though I now realise that not all versions have Perseus riding off on Pegasus, sometimes he uses winged shoes instead.) The Bellerophon part of the myth is not as well known, and I only discovered it myself in the last few years. One source I used is *Greek Myths* by Robert Graves (published by Penguin Books, 1955). There are so many different versions of the Greek myths, you can create your own favourite story from bits of all of them. That's what I do, anyway!

The Golden Horse
Gambian folktale

I really wanted a horse dung story for this collection, so I was delighted when I found this trickster tale, and I've already had a lot of fun telling it to audiences (shouting 'plop plop squelch' in a library is often the highlight of my day). The story of the golden dung is based on one episode from a longer story in *West African Folktales* by Jack Berry (published by Northwestern University Press, 1991).

Riddling for the Foal
Russian folktale

I'm a fan of riddles, so I love this story about a clever girl winning back her family's foal with her riddle answers and her no-nonsense attitude to the tsar. I first read it in *Russian Fairy Tales* by Alexsandr Afanas'ev, translated by Norbert Guterman (published by Pantheon Books, 1945). I've altered a few of the riddles asked by the tsar, so if you tell this story, you could make up your own riddles.

The Horse of Fire
Finnish myth

This is a very small slice of the amazing Finnish epic poem *Kalevala* translated by W.F. Kirby (published by Everyman's Library, 1907). I love the idea of a fiery horse being subdued by hail. In the original it's clear that Lemminkäinen breaks his promise not to hit the horse of fire, but it's not clear how the horse reacts. So I allowed the Fire Horse of Hiisi to get rid of the treacherous hero and go home to the meadow.

Flint Feet
Navajo myth

This is a beautiful story about the first horse, told by the Navajo people in North America. I first read it in *The Gift of the Gila Monster* by Gerald Hausman (Touchstone Books, 1993) and I have tried to stay true to the spirit of the story.

Bradamante and the Hippogriff
European legend

I first read about Bradamante in *Bulfinch's Mythology* by Thomas Bulfinch (published by Hamlyn, 1964). He retold stories about the Age of Chivalry and Charlemagne's knights from lots of sources, including Italian, French and German, so these were truly European heroes and heroines. My retelling is a small section of the massive epic legend, so I altered the beginning and end to make it work as a story on its own, and I also took out a few minor characters. But the female knight saving the male captive is totally genuine. As is the hippogriff.

The Unicorns and the Flood
Ukrainian folktale

I can't tell you what book I found this in, because I couldn't find a full version of the story. I read lots of different books about unicorns, and found lots of hints and glimpses of a Ukrainian story about the unicorn being too arrogant to join the other animals on the ark. But no matter how far I wandered through the forests of folklore tracking this elusive story, I couldn't find a genuine full Ukrainian version anywhere. However, that felt quite appropriate for a unicorn story, because unicorns themselves are notoriously difficult to find!

The Headless Horseman of New South Wales
Australian folktale

I first read a brief account of this ghostly horseman in *Horses In Australia, An Illustrated History* by Nicolas Brasch (published by NewSouth Publishing, 2014), then I broadened the story out with wider research. The ghost is a local celebrity, and the con-man butcher is also the star of some versions, but I couldn't find any information about why a man who drowned became a ghost without a head. And I have to admit I invented the statue in the town square. In real life, the story of the headless horseman is commemorated in a painting hanging in the pub in Booroorban...

The Kelpie with the Tangled Mane
Scottish folktale

As a Scottish writer and storyteller, I know a ridiculously large number of kelpie stories, but this is the first one I ever told and it's still one of my favourites, because I like the well-matched battle with the water bull. My version is adapted from an Islay tale in Volume 4 of *Popular Tales of the West Highlands* by J.F. Campbell (published by Edmonston and Douglas, 1862).

The Wise Colt
Jewish folktale

There are stories from all over the world about a helpful animal guiding a young man on a quest. I like this one, which I found in *Elijah's Violin and Other Jewish Folktales* by Howard Schwartz (published by Penguin Books, 1987) because the helpful animal is a wise talking horse. However, the original tale ends with the golden bird still trapped in the cage (though it's apparently content after being given a nice apple). One of the joys of retelling stories is that you can set the bird free if you want. And I did.

Fire and Clay
Indian tribal tale

This is an ancient creation story from the Munda tribal people of Chota Nagpur in India, which I found in *Folklore in the Old Testament* by James George Frazer (Macmillan, 1919). I love that a horse is the baddie and a spider is the goodie in this story.

Selling the Goddess
Tibetan tale

This is a small part of a much longer story about Goodheart and the tree goddess. I found it in *Tibetishe Märchen* by D. and M. Stovickova (translated from Czech to German by I. Kondrkova, published by Werner Dausien, 1974) and my very talented mother translated it from German to English for me. Thanks, Mum! However, she will undoubtedly be surprised at all the things I tweaked and removed, after her careful and precise translation. Sorry, Mum! (I lost the waving headscarf, but the tree, the snake, the cloud, the axe and, of course, the white horse all made it through...)

The Centaur's Heroes
Greek myth

I think centaurs are the most impressive horse-related fabled beasts, but they don't have many stories of their own, they tend to be bit players in other heroes' Greek myths. So I've stitched this Chiron story together from various Greek myths, including the stories in Charles Kingsley's *The Heroes*, or *Greek Fairy Tales for My Children* (published by Macmillan and Co, 1895), where I first read about Chiron's school for heroes. Though I did completely invent the birthday party. Centaurs usually crash weddings...

What You Learn at Wolf School
Balkan folktale

There are lots of brilliant folktales about little prey tricking large predators, but I enjoy this one because the prey is so much bigger than the predator. There are several old ballads from different parts of Europe which tell different versions of the 'horse kicks wolf' story, but I've been telling my own 'wolf school' story for so long I can't be sure which version inspired what element of my story. You can find one traditional version in *Tales from the Heart of the Balkans* by Bonnie C. Marshall and Vasa D. Mihailovich (published by Libraries Unlimited, 2001). When I tell this story in schools, I ask the audience to guess what the animal is, but I suspect in a book of horse stories, you all worked it out quite fast!

The Horse Who Fought a Lion
Persian legend

This is my favourite hero and horse story, which I found in the epic *Shahnameh, The Persian Book of Kings* written by Abolqasem Ferdowsi in the tenth century. (I read this English version: *Shahnameh*, translated by Dick Davies, published by Penguin Books, 2007.) My retelling is just the start of Rostam and Rakush's adventures, and I may have been kinder to the lion and the dragon than the original hero and his horse were.

Look out for more short story collections from Bloomsbury Education

BLOOMSBURY